It Was Kit

The 'True Story of Christopher Marlowe

By: Allison McWood

Annelid Press

It Was Kit: The 'True' Story of Christopher Marlowe
Copyright © 2020 by Allison McWood.
All rights reserved. No part of this book may be used or reproduced in any manner whatsoever without written permission except in the case of brief quotations embodied in critical articles and reviews. For information address Annelid Press. www.annelidpress.com.
FIRST EDITION

Cover photo by: Melissa-Jane Shaw

Edited by: Johnny Vong, Daniel Staheli

Featuring Original Cast Members: Kevin Risk, Kelsey Matheson, Chris Coculuzzi, Melissa-Jane Shaw, John Healy, Chantal Groulx

ISBN: 978-1-7771360-1-7

Cast List

KIT MARLOWE.......................................A playwright

THOMAS KYD ....His roommate

WILL SHAKESPEARE ....A playwright

ROBERT GREENE ....A playwright

INGRAM FRIZER ....A spy

NICHOLAS SKERES...............................A spy

BLOB POLEY..A spy

DICK BAINES..A counterfeiter

JOHN MARLOWE...................................Kit's father

CATHERINE ARTHUR ....Kit's mother

ANNE HATHAWAY ....Will's wife

ELEANOR BULL.....................................Owner of a rooming house

QUEEN ELIZABETH ....The Queen

DANBY...A coroner

OFFICER 1/ATHEIST 1/TAMBURLAINE

OFFICER 2/ATHEIST 2/FAUSTUS

Act One, Scene One

The apartment of KIT MARLOWE and THOMAS KYD.

THOMAS   Kit! *(enters)* There is a dead rat in my doublet. Why did you do it?

KIT   You're always blaming everything on me.

THOMAS   You're the only roommate I have, Kit. There's no one else to blame.

KIT   You know what your problem is, Thomas? You have no sense of humour.

THOMAS   I fail to see the humour in finding dead vermin in my clothing.

KIT   I wanted to see what your reaction would be.

THOMAS   This is so like you. I don't understand why you find entertainment in making me furious with... What are you doing?

KIT   Cleaning up.

THOMAS   Who are you and what have you done with Kit?

KIT   My parents are coming to visit.

THOMAS   Good Ud, no.

KIT   Would you shut your yap and give me a hand?

Knock at the door.

KIT   That couldn't be them already. *(answers door)* Will.

WILL   I brought the script!

KIT   Will, this is not a good time.

WILL   If I have to wait any longer to work on a play with you, I might soil myself.

THOMAS   Pleasant. Now if you gentlemen will excuse me, I'm going to dispose of this rat. *(exits)*

WILL   I was up all night working on this draft. Tell me what you think.

KIT   Listen, Will. I don't have much time left.

WILL   Just skim it. I'll be forever in your debt.

KIT   Will!

WILL   I look up to you! You are so brave! So innovative. So...so well dressed!

KIT   Will...

WILL   You are three months my elder, but eons ahead of me in insight.

KIT   Will...

WILL   I want to BE you!

KIT   No you don't.

WILL   I want to think like you, dress like you, but most of all I want to write plays the way you do. Please help me with my play.

KIT   I don't have ti...

WILL   *(getting on his knees)* I am your spaniel!

KIT   Will, please, no. Not the spaniel thing again.

WILL   (sitting up like a dog) Bark.

KIT   Will, this is not necess...

WILL   Bark.

KIT   Your embarrassing yoursel...

WILL   Bark.

KIT   For the love of Ud, Will! Don't make me hurt you!

WILL   Whimper.

KIT   *(sigh)* What's the working title.

WILL   Oh! I knew I could count on you, Kit! Because that's the
                kind of guy you are!

KIT   Don't hug me. What's the working title?

WILL   Romeo and Juliet.

KIT   ...Right.

WILL   Go ahead. Skim...Skim, skim, skim.

                                    As KIT skims through the script, he
                                    tries to suppress laughter. WILL
                                    absorbs KIT's every expression.
                                    KIT lets out a stifled chortle.

WILL   What? What's funny? What?

KIT   It's...cute.

WILL   Cute? I wasn't going for cute. But cute's good. Now is
                that your honest opinion?

KIT   Not entirely.

WILL   Be merciful, Kit! I'm dying here! Tell me what you really
                think! I can take it! What!

KIT   This is the corniest play I have ever read in my life.

WILL	What?
KIT	Will, this play stinks of cheese.
WILL	What's wrong with it?
KIT	It's fluff. It's mushy. It's a girl's play. What are you? A girl?
WILL	I don't know what to say.
KIT	I would never write a play like this.
WILL	It's a love story.
KIT	I don't write about love. I write about hatred.
WILL	And that's what's so endearing about you. Maybe if we collaborated...
KIT	I can't. You know how vain I am. To collaborate would mean I would have to share the credit and that is totally out of character for me. Besides, this is your play.
WILL	OUR play.
KIT	No, Will. It's yours. I can't put my name on this. It's not my style. Sure, there's slaughter and suicide. And I approve of that. But there's not enough destruction. It's not over-the-top. It's not dangerous.
WILL	I can be dangerous! I can be dangerous like you! We

have a lot more in common than you think.

KIT   Will, pay attention. We are not...the same...person.

WILL   Oh, fie.

                                    ROBERT invites himself in.

ROBERT   Greetings, Christopher! How is the best dressed playwright in England?

KIT   I'm well, Robert...Wait a minute. Didn't you die last year?

ROBERT   I dropped by to see if my favourite colleague would like to join me at the tavern where we can have drinks and discuss how obscenely intelligent we are.

WILL   May I come too, Mr. Greene?

ROBERT   What is he doing here? Who let him in?

KIT   Both of you, please! I'm running out of time!

ROBERT   *(to WILL)* Thou tripe! Thou disease! Thou uneducated eel!

WILL   Please stop calling me 'thou.' It makes me uncomfortable.

ROBERT   Christopher, what did I tell you about fraternizing with swine? Ignorance is contagious, you know.

WILL   I agree with you, Mr. Greene.

KIT   He's filling theatres.

WILL   Can't argue with you there.

ROBERT   I wouldn't stand in the penny yard to watch his drivel.

WILL   I don't blame you.

KIT   I agree his plays are fluffy, but the rest of England seems to like them.

WILL   Absolutely.

ROBERT   He's not like us, Christopher. He didn't go to Cambridge. He's not part of the educated elite. Who does he think he is, hogging our audiences? Pure travesty!

WILL   He has a point, Kit.

KIT   Will, you can't keep agreeing with both of us.

WILL   I couldn't agree with you more.

KIT   Will...

WILL   I don't want to offend anyone.

ROBERT   *(to WILL)* Heed my warning. Keep your hindquarters out of the theatre! You don't belong here! Just because everyone loves your plays, doesn't mean they are any good.

KIT   You know something, Robert? You really should unwedge whatever it is you have stuck up your arse. And do it before my parents arrive.

WILL   Your parents are coming! How lovely! Can I stay and visit?

KIT   Absolutely not. Both of you, out!

Knock at the door.

KIT   You see? My parents are here already and not only am I ill prepared, I've got you two fops lingering around like a foul odour...Mom? Dad? Is that you?

DICK   *(from outside)* It's me!

KIT   It's Richard Baines! Hide!

Everyone hides.

DICK   I know you're in there! Open up, will you?

KIT reluctantly opens the door.

KIT   Dick.

DICK   I go by Richard, actually. People don't call me Dick.

KIT   That's what you think.

DICK   Robert. Will. Make yourselves scarce. I have something of great importance to discuss with Kit.

WILL   We were just leaving.

ROBERT   If there's one thing you can do, Dick, it's clear a room.

Exit WILL and ROBERT

DICK   Mind if I help myself to some ale? Don't mind if I do.

Helps himself to ale.

KIT   Don't drink that! I'll have nothing to offer my parents!

DICK   Didn't your parents teach you to share?

KIT   What was I thinking? I'm sure my parents won't mind drinking from the chamber pot.

DICK   Let's get down to business. Kit, I like you. Hang me, I LIKE you. That's why I'm letting you in on a little business negotiation. Kit, how would you like to...

KIT   No.

DICK   I can make you a wealthy man. Think of it, Kit. You could move out of this seedy neighbourhood. And think of all the pretty clothes you could buy.

KIT   I like living in the Liberties, and my brother-in-law is a tailor.

DICK   Let me explain something to you...

KIT   You've been counterfeiting again, haven't you?

DICK   Don't call it counterfeiting. It makes me sound dishonest.

KIT   I'll none of it, Dick. You've gotten me in trouble with the law in the past for illicit coining. You will not cozen me into it again.

DICK   This ale is horrible. *(dumps ale on the floor)*

KIT   Dick! I have an urge to crack this bottle over your skull!

DICK   Take a number. So, can I call you a partner?

KIT   You are not to be trusted.

DICK   You're overreacting.

KIT   You tried to wipe out an entire seminary by poisoning their drinking water.

DICK   Come on, Kit! The Queen is after me again. I need someone to help me save face, and you are the smartest man I know!

KIT   Out!

                                        KIT pushes DICK out the door. KIT leaves the room.

DICK   *(from outside)* Kit! I'll make it worth your while! Kit!...Kit?

                                        When KIT does not answer, DICK opens the door and peaks around the corner. Once he sees that no one is around, he sneaks into the apartment and hides in a cupboard.

Act One, Scene Two

> *INGRAM, NICHOLAS AND BLOB are hiding in the bushes outside KIT's apartment.*

INGRAM   What's he doing now?

BLOB   *(looking through the window)* He's wiping a puddle of ale from the floor.

NICHOLAS   How can an ex-spy lead such a boring life?

BLOB   Hey. This is Christopher Marlowe we're talking about. Give him some time. He'll eventually do something offensive.

NICHOLAS   Who would have guessed we would ever get to spy on a former colleague?

BLOB   I'm confused. Why does the Queen want us to spy on Kit?

INGRAM   The Queen heard a rumour that Marlowe is a double agent. She's afraid for her life.

NICHOLAS   How a propos. The three of us spying on a suspected double agent. We, being double agents ourselves.

Blob, do you remember the year of 1586?

NICHOLAS & BLOB *(dreamily)* The Babington Plot.

INGRAM   I missed that one.

BLOB   How could you possibly miss the Babington Plot?

NICHOLAS   Don't you have any experience in intelligence work?

INGRAM   I have no record of intelligence.

NICHOLAS   But it was the BABINGTON Plot!

BLOB   Oh, Ingram, it was thrilling! You should have been there!

NICHOLAS   Espionage at its finest!

BLOB   We plotted against the Queen's life in an attempt to...

NICHOLAS   ...replace her with Mary Queen of ...

BLOB   ...Scots! And all of the conspirators were executed.

NICHOLAS   Except us, of course.

BLOB   Because we're sneaky.

INGRAM   I envy you, gentlemen. Nothing is more amusing than split loyalties.

NICHOLAS   Don't feel bad, Ingram. You're not a bad little liar yourself.

INGRAM   Oh, Nicholas. You're just saying that.

NICHOLAS   Come on, Mr. Conny-Catching Loan Shark. What about all those unassuming, rich gentlemen you cheated. You should see this guy in action, Blob. He's brilliant. He charges wealthy gentlemen one hundred percent interest on their loans. If they can't pay the interest, he forfeits their property. And here's the kicker. The loans are never forthcoming.

BLOB   You jest.

NICHOLAS   If I speak the truth, may I never tell a lie again. I'm a big fan of Ingram's work. It's a hobby of mine to act as his frequent accomplice. You would be proud, Blob. I am the one who identifies and lures those foolish gentlemen into Ingram's trap.

INGRAM   I couldn't do it without you, Nicholas.

BLOB   I'll admit, it takes savvy to be a moneylender, but it takes pure genius to be a pathological liar.

NICHOLAS   He's got you there, Ingram. Blob has mastered the art of lying. He is a most cunning counterfeiter and dissembler. A notable knave with no trust in him.

BLOB   Oh! You flatter me!

INGRAM   Are you telling me you're pathological?

BLOB   Would I lie about something like that?

INGRAM   Prove it.

BLOB   Okay. I will...I am fond of the Queen.

NICHOLAS   Oh! That was a good one, Blob! You really had me going there for a minute.

BLOB   Notice how I looked you straight in the face when I said that? Not a flinch.

INGRAM   Not bad. I wasn't entirely convinced, but...

BLOB   What do you mean you were not entirely convinced? I can lie convincingly under any circumstances. I can look the Queen herself right in the eyes and lie to her ugly face. And I have! On more than one occasion. What about the Babington Plot?

INGRAM   Would you let it go? That stupid Babington Plot was over a long time ago!

BLOB   What's his problem?

NICHOLAS   Don't brag too much about being a better liar than Ingram. He's a bit sensitive about that.

BLOB   Fie on me. Listen, Ingram, I'm sorry. You are every bit as good a liar as I am.

NICHOLAS   Damn, he's good! Blob Poley, you are the master!

INGRAM   Oh! For the love of Ud!

Act One, Scene Three

KIT is wiping ale from the floor in his apartment. Enter THOMAS.

KIT   It's about time. I could have used your help, you know.

THOMAS   They're your parents.

KIT   What took you so long, anyway? How long could it take to dispose of a dead rat?

THOMAS   I didn't exactly dispose of him.

KIT   Him? Since when did this dead rat go from being an it to a him?

THOMAS   Stuff happens.

KIT   So if you didn't dispose of the rat, what did you do?

THOMAS   I took him to the tavern.

KIT   What for?

THOMAS   Drinks.

KIT   You took a dead rat to the tavern?

THOMAS   Could you please not call him the dead rat anymore?
            His name is Stiffy.

KIT   You named him?

THOMAS   I was going to get rid of him. I was! I went to the
            riverbank, took Stiffy by the tail and was just about to
            fling him, when something came over me. I looked into
            his little face. And...well...I sort of felt sorry for him. I
            realized that I could relate to this rat. I am a lot like this
            rat. This rat and I have a lot in common.

KIT   In what sense?

THOMAS   I've invited Stiffy to live here with us, Kit. I told him you
            wouldn't mind.

KIT   You are not keeping a dead rat in our apartment.

THOMAS   His name is Stiffy.

KIT   Thomas, that rat is going to decompose and start to
            stink.

THOMAS   Someday you'll decompose and start to stink.

KIT   Yes, but when that happens, I don't plan on living here.

THOMAS   Kit, this is something I have to do. Whenever I look at
            this rat, I get this weird feeling. I feel overcome with
            guilt.

KIT   Guilt?

THOMAS   I wasn't there for Stiffy when he was alive. I want to spend the rest of my life making it up to him.

KIT   That's noble, Thomas. But my parents will be arriving soon, and if there is a dead rat in the apartment, it will be yet another thing for us to fight about.

THOMAS   He'll behave.

Knock at the door.

KIT   That must be my parents. Hide that thing, will you?

KIT answers the door to reveal two men.

ATHEIST 1   Good afternoon. We represent the London chapter of the Atheist Brigade. Our mission is to go door to door, spreading atheism to misinformed Christians. Are you a misinformed Christian?

KIT   I'm afraid you're wasting your time.

ATHEIST 2   That's where you're wrong. We are the bearers of good news. Wouldn't you like to live with the peace of mind that when you die, absolutely nothing will happen?

ATHEIST 1   And won't it be easier to sleep at night knowing that the earth is being randomly hurled around in space with no higher power to keep it secure?

KIT   I'm not listening. I...

ATHEIST 2 Atheism promises an eternity of nothingness, along with a satisfying void that most people so mindlessly fill with spirituality.

ATHEIST 1 Would you like to share in our joy as we experience this void together?

KIT   You understand that what you are doing is a felony.

ATHEIST 2 We are doing it for the greater good.

ATHEIST 1 It will only take a moment of your time. All you have to do is join hands with us now and say the Sinner's Prayer backwards.

KIT   You can't tell me what to believe!

ATHEIST 2 This poor man has a soul. It makes me all weepy.

ATHEIST 1 Why don't we just leave you these brochures. Perhaps if you read them, you will come to your senses and change your mind. Good day.

ATHEIST 2 *(on their way out)* And you can be assured that neither one of us will be praying for you.

Exit Atheists.

THOMAS What was that all about?

KIT   It was the Atheist Brigade. They left us more of this bloody, Atheist literature.

THOMAS   Again?

KIT   Just put it in the closet with the rest of them.

Knock at the door.

KIT   Those Atheists never give up! *(answers door)* How many times do I have to tell you, I am not an Atheist!

JOHN   That's good to know.

KIT   Mom. Dad.

Exit THOMAS.

JOHN   Good to see you, Son. *(hands KIT shoes)* Here. Have some shoes.

CATHERINE   My adorable, baby boy!

JOHN   So, Kit. When are you going to get a real job?

KIT   Congratulations, Dad. It only took you twelve seconds this time.

CATHERINE   Have you met a nice girl yet, Kitty?

KIT   Mom...

JOHN   Shoes. That's where the money is, son. Everyone needs shoes. You are a Marlowe, and Marlowe men make shoes.

KIT   I've been doing well for myself. The Admiral's Men have been performing some of my work. In fact, they're doing *Dr. Faustus* right now. I was going to invite you to...

JOHN   *Dr. Faustus?* Is that the play with the Jew, the racist, the devil or the queer?

KIT   YOU read my work?

JOHN   Your mother says I should be supportive. So which is it?

KIT   The one with the devil.

JOHN   My son. The devil-lover.

KIT   I do not love the devil.

JOHN   No. You just write plays about him.

KIT   There are nuns in *The Jew of Malta*. Does that make me a nun?

JOHN   Apparently not if you go around writing plays about the devil.

CATHERINE   You can meet lots of nice people selling shoes, Kitty. Lady people.

KIT   I don't want to be a shoemaker!

JOHN   Would you listen to that, Catherine? My first born son would rather prance around on a stage in his leotards than take me up on the invaluable shoe empire I built for him. What's wrong, Kit? You too good to be a Marlowe?

CATHERINE   There is no shame in shoe business. Your father is a member of the Shoemaker and Tanner's Guild.

KIT   What in frigging hell am I going to do with a profuse education in Classical Literature if I'm making shoes?

JOHN   Don't think education makes you better than a shoemaker, because it doesn't, you pompous, little brat!

KIT   You think I'M pompous? Ever since you became a clerk at St. Mary's, you strut around like you're some sort of evangelist!

DICK   (peaking from the cupboard, writing something down) John the Evangelist.

CATHERINE   (lets out a scream) The agony! The agony! To see my two best boys fighting like mongrels in the street! Woe is me! Woe! Woe!

JOHN   Stop being so dramatic, Catherine.

CATHERINE   You two used to be as close-knit as netherstocks. John, do you remember when Kitty was wee? He was so afraid of thunder, he used to crawl into bed with you on stormy nights. Remember how cute he was?

DICK   *(writing)* ...Bedfellow to John the Evangelist.

KIT   Nobody, not even my own father can tell me how to live my life. I am a free thinker!

JOHN   You're not old enough to be a free thinker. You're only twelve years old!

KIT   I'm twenty-nine!

JOHN   As far as your mother and I are concerned, you're twelve!

CATHERINE   Kitty, why is there a hole in your wall?

THOMAS   *(entering)* It was Kit.

KIT   Thomas, go away.

THOMAS   Kit got mad and put his fist through the wall.

KIT   There you go, blaming me again.

THOMAS   Kit has a vicious temper.

JOHN   Must get it from his mother's side.

CATHERINE   I'm worried, Kitty.

KIT   Oh, here we go.

CATHERINE   We have discussed your tantrums before.

KIT   Mom...

CATHERINE   And another thing. I don't think I approve of this neighborhood you live in.

KIT   What's wrong with the Liberties?

CATHERINE   On our way here we saw two very friendly young ladies who were almost completely naked.

JOHN   Arrroooo!

CATHERINE   I'm worried.

KIT   There's nothing to worry about.

CATHERINE   I'm concerned they might be cold. Maybe you should loan them some of your clothes, Kitty. You always have such nice clothes.

JOHN   And where, might I ask did you get the money to purchase such lavish attire? Answer me, Mr. Fancy-Pants. Where does a playwright find that kind of money?

THOMAS   He and Dick Baines were involved in a counterfeiting scheme a couple of years back.

KIT   You little snitch!

CATHERINE   Dick Baines. I don't approve of him, Kitty. He's a bad influence.

DICK	*(inside cupboard, speaking in stage whisper)* That's not true! You dishonest wench!
JOHN	My son is a counterfeiting bastard!
DICK	*(writing)* ...Bastard. His mother dishonest.
JOHN	What other trouble has my son been getting into, Thomas?
THOMAS	Not much. Unless you count the time he was arrested for murder.
JOHN	What!
CATHERINE	*(face down, pounding her fists on the floor)* Lordy! Lordy! Lordy! I've given birth to a murderer!
KIT	I wasn't charged!
THOMAS	He started a tavern brawl.
KIT	Why is it that every time I happen to be present at a tavern brawl, everyone thinks I'm the one who started it?
THOMAS	I don't know, Kit. Could it be your lewd mouth and violent temper?
KIT	I never hurt anyone.
THOMAS	He's always attempting sudden privy injury to men.

KIT   It's my sharp tongue that causes injury.

JOHN   So, about this brawl...

KIT   I was trying to break it up! Watson the poet got in a tiff with Bradley the inn-keeper's son. I tried to...

JOHN   So it was a poet. It's always a poet.

CATHERINE   Why can't you be more like Will Shakespeare? He's such a nice boy.

KIT   Mother...

CATHERINE   He's married, Kitty. And has three children.

KIT   Come on, Mom! Two of them are twins. They only count as one.

CATHERINE   Level with me, Kitty. Will I ever be a grandmother?

KIT   Stop pressuring me!

CATHERINE   Is something not functioning? Do you need to see a doctor?

KIT   That's enough!

CATHERINE   Why, Kitty? All I want to know is why? Why are you denying me my fundamental right to watch my son crank out miniature versions of himself?

KIT   It's my business!

CATHERINE   Why?

KIT   Because I...

CATHERINE   Why?

KIT   It's not what I...

CATHERINE   Why...

KIT   Because I...Because...Because I prefer men. That's it. I prefer men.

THOMAS   Holy crap!

DICK   *(writing vigorously)* This is too easy.

KIT   Mother? Mother, speak to me.

CATHERINE   I've failed! I've failed! I've failed!

JOHN   *(stuffing a shoe in her mouth)* Stuff it, Catherine.

KIT   That's right. This is why I'm not married. And anyone who loves not tobacco and boys are fools.

DICK   *(writing)* You are so quotable, Kit.

JOHN   *(taking KIT aside)* Son, can I have a word with you a moment? *(cuffs him on the head)* Have you fallen on your head?

KIT   What!

JOHN   You're queer, just like that king in your play!

            *CATHERINE swoons and falls into
            THOMAS' arms. THOMAS tends to
            her.*

JOHN   You know what they do with queers? They use them
            for kindling, that's what they do!

KIT   Dad, I am not gay!

JOHN   But you just said that...

KIT   I said that so Mom would stop harassing me to get
            married.

JOHN   You lied to your mother.

KIT   It wasn't a lie...exactly...It was more...irony.

JOHN   Don't use those fancy Cambridge words with me, boy. I
            know a lie when I hear one.

KIT   It's not a fancy Cambridge word. It's irony. I was being
            ironic. I was saying the opposite of what I mean to
            make a point.

JOHN   Sounds like a lie to me.

KIT   It's a playwriting technique.

JOHN   Well, here's a shoemaker's technique. Say what you mean! This irony as you call it, is going to land you in serious trouble! You mark my words! Now where are you taking us for dinner?

KIT   *(sigh)* Get your cloaks.

                                              Exit KIT and JOHN. THOMAS drags CATHERINE out. Once everyone is gone, DICK comes out of the cupboard and speaks to the audience.

DICK   I've got it all here, in my own handwriting. This will create quite a diversion. The Queen won't waste her time interrogating a meager counterfeiter when there is a blaspheming heathen right under her nose. Marlowe will be sorry he didn't help me out with my ploy. How sweet it is to savour revenge while simultaneously keeping my arse from being hanged. Might as well break two heads with one mace.

THOMAS   *(re-entering)* Are you talking to yourself again, Dick?

DICK   Thomas! No one was here, so I let myself in. I peed in the corner. I hope you don't mind.

THOMAS   Why have you plagued us with your presence?

DICK   I was looking for something.

THOMAS   Did you find it?

DICK   Oh, yes. I did.

ACT ONE, SCENE FOUR

A tavern. WILL is seated at a table with KIT. WILL has a quill and paper. KIT has his head buried in his arms.

KIT   Wench! More ale!

WILL   So about Romeo and Juliet.

KIT   Another time, Will.

WILL   But I...

Enter ROBERT.

ROBERT   What ho! Christopher! How pleasant to...*(sees WILL)* What is the meaning of this?

KIT   Moan.

ROBERT   This is OUR table, Christopher! This is where the two of us sit and discuss lofty matters. What could a famous gracer of tragedians be doing here with this maggot?

KIT   My head is swimming. *(flops head back in his arms)*

ROBERT   *(to WILL)* Thou virus. Thou flea. Thou illiterate bard.

WILL   Would you like to read my play, Mr. Greene?

ROBERT   I've read your work, Shakespeare. And I've seen more tantalizing morsels in my own vomit.

WILL   I'm sure you had a good reason for saying that.

ROBERT   I warned you to stop infecting our theatres with this brain-numbing puke you so you so ignorantly refer to as drama.

WILL   I value your opinion, Mr. Greene. But nonetheless, people seem to be swarming like flies to see my plays.

ROBERT   Flies don't swarm to theatres. They swarm around in circles until they find manure to land on.

WILL   That is a clever analogy.

ROBERT   I deserve success, not you! I will give you one last chance. Go back to Stratford where you belong!

WILL   But...

ROBERT   You are no genius. *(pulls KIT's head up by the hair, revealing KIT making a stupid, drunk face)* Now THIS is the face of a genius.

WILL   I never said I was a genius. I'm just an ordinary guy who likes writing plays.

ROBERT   They are not plays. They are shallow puddles. Away with you, thou ruffian. Thou mongrel. Thou menstrual rag!

WILL   That reminds me. I need to send a missive to my wife. My twins are having a birthday.

                              Exit WILL. ROBERT sits next to KIT.

ROBERT   Christopher?

KIT   Grunt.

ROBERT   Shakespeare must be destroyed.

KIT   Sure thing, Robert.

ROBERT   I did not pursue a higher education only to skulk in the shadow of that buffoon.

KIT   Belch.

ROBERT   I heard that Shakespeare has taken an interest in writing sonnets. Well, so have I.

KIT   Sssonnets.

ROBERT   I have written a collection of 154 sonnets, and have signed Shakespeare's name on them.

KIT   Lots of pretty sonnets.

ROBERT   Oh, these are better than anything Shakespeare could ever write. Especially the ones a about the mistress.

KIT   Are you sure you're not dead?

ROBERT   I'm sure there's a little lady in Stratford who would like
             to read these sonnets. Surely she would like to know
             what her loyal husband is up to.

KIT   Need ale.

ROBERT   I'm sending my masterpiece to Stratford. Today.
             Shakespeare will wish he had heeded my warning.

ACT ONE, SCENE FIVE

INGRAM, NICHOLAS and BLOB are in the bushes.

INGRAM   Someone's coming!

                DICK enters. There is a disappointed moan among the spies.

DICK   What are you guys doing in the bushes?

BLOB   We could tell you, but then we'd have to kill you.

NICHOLAS   That's not a bad idea, actually.

BLOB   Good point. We have been sent to spy on Christopher Marlowe.

DICK   Spies? Do you work for the Queen?

NICHOLAS   At times.

INGRAM   Let's kill him now.

DICK   Before you kill me, I have something that could be of some value to you.

BLOB   What say you?

DICK   I have evidence that Christopher Marlowe is a heretic.
                A homosexual one at that.

INGRAM   Solid evidence?

DICK   Define solid.

NICHOLAS   This is not a game, little man. The Queen isn't going to
                be interested in flimsy evidence.

DICK   I was hiding in Marlowe's cupboard and I wrote down
                everything he said.

INGRAM   *(taking notes from DICK)* Let me see this...I don't
                understand your shorthand. You keep writing a capital
                letter 'C.' What does the capital letter 'C' signify?

DICK   You are spies. You figure it out.

                                    *Exit DICK. The spies examine the
                                    notes.*

INGRAM   The capital letter 'C.'

NICHOLAS   You morons. It must stand for Christopher.

BLOB   Or Christ.

INGRAM   Blob has a point. 'Christopher' makes no sense in the
                context. 'Christ' sounds better. Listen to this..."A note
                regarding the opinion of one Christopher Marlowe

concerning his damnable judgement of religion and scorn of God's word." He says "that St. John the Evangelist was bedfellow to 'C.' That 'C' was a bastard and his mother dishonest."

BLOB   Didn't I tell you? That filthy heathen is talking about Christ!

INGRAM   And down here it says "all they that love not tobacco and boys are fools."

NICHOLAS   Did Marlowe really say that?

BLOB   What difference does it make? We have it written down.

NICHOLAS   It's payday, Gentelmen! Let's take this to the Queen.

INGRAM   Not so fast. What we hold in our hands is blasphemy. An overt attack on God. If the Queen finds this in our possession...

NICHOLAS   She'll think it's an attack on her. Because she thinks she is God.

INGRAM   She might assume that we had something to do with this.

BLOB   We'll be accused of treason.

NICHOLAS   And hanged.

INGRAM   And that won't look too good on our record.

BLOB   So what do we do?

INGRAM   These notes need to be found in Marlowe's possession.
              We'll plant them in his apartment.

NICHOLAS   We'll go to the Queen and tell her we have reason to
              believe that Marlowe is plotting treason.

BLOB   We'll request that she issue a search warrant.

INGRAM   They'll find the notes.

NICHOLAS   And the Queen will give us a beefy raise.

BLOB   This is such fun!

Act One, Scene Six

The apartment. KIT is lying limply in a chair.

THOMAS   Stiffy wants to know why you never told us that you prefer men. He feels that if he is going to live here with us, he has a right to be informed of any major liabilities.

KIT   That rat has a lot to say.

THOMAS   You're not being fair to Stiffy.

KIT   If Stiffy wasn't already dead, I'd...

THOMAS   You are so temperamental.

KIT   I wouldn't be temperamental if I wasn't surrounded by so many irritating people.

THOMAS   I can understand why you didn't tell Stiffy. You hardly know him. But why didn't you tell me? Did you think I would think less of you? Did you think I would turn you in?

KIT   I am not gay.

THOMAS   You're not gay? OH. This is so like you.

KIT   Brace yourself. I feel a sarcastic insult coming on.

THOMAS   This is one of your pranks, isn't it? You're going around saying you're gay just to see how many people you can get a rise out of.

KIT   Not exactly. But those would be happy results.

THOMAS   Don't deny it. I know you. Everything you do has to be like a wet fish in the face. Over the top. Larger than life. Shocking! This sort of thing may work in your plays, but its annoying as hell when you have to live with it day after day!

KIT   I'm about due for a public disturbance. May I leave now, or would that be rude?

THOMAS   You have got to stop living as though you are a character in one of your plays.

KIT   I don't do that.

THOMAS   Good Ud! Sometimes I think you have completely confused reality with drama. Isn't that right, Stiffy?

                    KIT throws STIFFY out the window.

KIT   You want to be next?

THOMAS   I can't believe you just did that.

KIT   The rat had it coming.

THOMAS   You're trying to make me mad.

KIT   It's so easy to do.

THOMAS   I'm having a nervous breakdown!

KIT   I'm having a hangover. Want to trade?

THOMAS   You are impossible!

KIT   You haven't shut up yet.

THOMAS   I am going to retrieve Stiffy.

KIT   Don't bother coming back.

                                   Exit THOMAS.

KIT   Ah! Solitude!

                                   TAMBURLAINE appears.

TAMBURLAINE He's right, you know.

KIT   Not you again.

TAMBURLAINE I'm in your imagination. You can't escape me.

KIT   Even in my imagination I can't find peace.

TAMBURLAINE   Peace? You? The king of civil unrest?

KIT   Listen, Tamburlaine, I wrote you and I can erase you.

TAMBURLAINE   You can't. I'm part of who you are.

KIT   I am nothing like you.

TAMBURLAINE   Thomas was right. You are synonymous with the characters in your plays.

KIT   I am not a sadistic killer like yourself! I never killed anyone!

TAMBURLAINE   You didn't have to. I did it for you.

KIT   Tamburlaine...

TAMBURLAINE   We are the same. Face it. We're both overreachers. Grabbing what we want.

KIT   I worked hard for everything I have!

TAMBURLAINE   You were a shoemaker's son. I was a shepherd. You think no one will make the connection?

KIT   You don't understand. I...

TAMBURLAINE   You want to be the Father of Drama. To brand your insignia on the theatre's flank. To change the very essence of dramatic literature as we know it.

KIT   So what's wrong with...

TAMBURLAINE   I want to rule the world.

KIT   You're just as bad as everyone else, you know that? You think you have me figured out because of the plays I write. That's not fair.

TAMBURLAINE   You mean to tell me that parts of yourself never end up in your characters? You are lying to yourself.

KIT   You don't know me. You don't know anything about me! Nobody does!

TAMBURLAINE   I know you as well as I know myself. We are the same, only I'm better.

KIT   What the...

TAMBURLAINE   You made me a hero.

KIT   I made you a burlesque. I was making fun of...

TAMBURLAINE   People think I'm a hero.

KIT   Only because they don't understand what I was trying to do. I was trying something different. Nobody has ever done this sort of thing before.

TAMBURLAINE   Irony is dangerous, Marlowe. Of late, people have posted racist threats on church doors, and have done it in the name of Tamburlaine.

KIT   I have no control over how people react to my work.

TAMBURLAINE Your efforts have backfired.

KIT   Out, scab! Get out of my mind!

TAMBURLAINE It's too late. I am in control now. I have taken possession of your thoughts. You will never escape. Stoop thou, and be footstool to great Tamburlaine!

KIT   NO!

FAUSTUS appears.

FAUSTUS   Why don't you just leave him alone?

TAMBURLAINE Faustus?

FAUSTUS   Like the poor guy hasn't been through enough as it is. Marlowe, I know exactly how you feel.

KIT   I will not stand here and be defended by a fictitious character.

FAUSTUS   Would you look at that? He's in denial. I was in denial once.

KIT   Denial?

FAUSTUS   Denial about selling your soul to the devil.

KIT   I did no such thing.

FAUSTUS   Poor wretch. Do you want a hug? Here. Let me give you a hug.

KIT   Why are you hugging me?

FAUSTUS   I am comforting you in the last meager moments you have on this earth. You are going straight to hell.

KIT   What say you?

FAUSTUS   You sold your soul to the devil.

KIT   That wasn't me. That was you.

FAUSTUS   When you were at Cambridge you renounced everything that was important to you for the sake of acquiring knowledge. You gave up your family.

KIT   I wanted more than the life of a simple shoemaker.

FAUSTUS   You prostituted your morals.

KIT   What morals?

FAUSTUS   You worked as a spy to put yourself through school.

KIT   Students always get the shit jobs.

FAUSTUS   You gave up on God.

KIT   The church disappointed me. Not God.

FAUSTUS   Was it worth it? Was it worth selling your soul for knowledge?

KIT   Why must you insist...

TAMBURLAINE   Maybe YOU are a character in a play. Ever think of that, Marlowe? Who's to say you are not the product of someone's imagination.

FAUSTUS   Don't freak him out.

TAMBURLAINE   Marlowe, your life is no different than any of the twisted plots you thought up. Do you think someone wrote YOU?

FAUSTUS   Listen, you verbose bag of self-importance, there is no point in worsening his lot. His time is almost up.

KIT   What do you mean by that?

> *TAMBURLAINE and FAUSTUS disappear.*

KIT   What do you mean my time is...Faustus? Tamburlaine!

Act One, Scene Seven

INGRAM is alone in the bushes.

INGRAM   Every man must leave his mark. What about me? True, I am a lewd moneylender. A shark. I disrupt the lives of cocky, young gentlemen. But it's not the Babington Plot. Nicholas, Blob and that bloody Babington Plot. How can I compete with that? Then there's Marlowe with his controversial plays and public disturbances. That lucky bugger has trouble just falling in his lap. People will remember Marlowe and Nicholas and Blob. When I'm buried, my name will just vaporize and no one will ever remember I was alive. *(enter NICHOLAS)* What ho! Is the deed done?

NICHOLAS   It was too easy. I slipped into Marlowe's apartment and left the scandalous notes in his closet.

INGRAM   Good, good.

NICHOLAS   He was so engrossed in a conversation with William Shakespeare that neither one noticed I was there.

BLOB rushes in.

BLOB   The Queen has been informed!

NICHOLAS   Blob, you are a marvel!

BLOB   I looked the Queen straight in the face and told her about Marlowe's treacherous plottings. She turned a revolting shade of green!

NICHOLAS   Blob, I could hug you.

BLOB   Please don't.

INGRAM   I could have lied to the Queen too, you know. Hell, I could have planted the notes in Marlowe's closet. But instead, I was left alone in the bushes, twiddling my thumbs.

NICHOLAS   But you are so good at things like that.

BLOB   Excellent twiddling.

INGRAM   You don't think I'm a good spy.

NICHOLAS   Of course we do.

INGRAM   Enough of your pretense! I know what the two of you think of me. You think I'm a half ass spy with the balls of a neutered cat! I'll not be made to look like a court jester! I AM A SPY!

                            ROBERT walks by and gives INGRAM a weird look.

NICHOLAS   Nice going, Ingram.

BLOB   What part of SECRET agent confuses you?

INGRAM   Fie.

Act One, Scene Eight

> *WILL and KIT are in KIT's apartment.*

WILL   How do fairies sound to you? Fairies frolicking in the forest, causing mischief among young lovers. Wouldn't fairies be fun, Kit?

KIT   Do your characters ever talk to you?

WILL   What say you?

KIT   The characters in your plays. Do they talk to you?

WILL   Titus Andronicus once appeared to me in a dream and slapped me. Then I remembered he didn't have a hand. But it made so much sense when I was dreaming it.

KIT   I'm not talking about dreams, Will. I mean, do your characters walk into your apartment and speak to you the way I'm speaking to you now?

WILL   Has this happened to you? OH! Your imagination puts me to shame!

KIT   Do you think about death?

WILL   I don't have much time to die, really. I busy myself mostly with living.

KIT   Surely you ponder death occasionally.

WILL   No. Living pretty much consumes most of my schedule.

                              ROBERT enters, smirking.

KIT   Robert? Why are you looking so smug?

ROBERT   No reason.

                              ROBERT points to the door at the exact moment someone knocks.

WILL   Are you expecting someone, Kit?

ANNE   *(from outside)* Open up! I know you're in there, you double crossing bag of horse plop!

KIT   Will, is that your wife?

WILL   Anne? Is that you, my angelic one?

ANNE   Damn straight, it's me! Now open this door so I can break your head!

WILL   How wonderful! My little flower has journeyed all the way from Stratford to surprise me!

                              WILL opens the door. As ANNE storms in, ROBORT stands aside and gloats.

ANNE   I thought I might find you here, you little wank!

WILL   I'm sure you meant that affectionately.

ANNE   Where is she?

WILL   She who?

ANNE   That little whore you've been slamming!

WILL   I'm confused.

ANNE   How could you do this to me? How could you do this to
                little Judith and Hamnet?

WILL   Do what?

ANNE   You leave me alone in Stratford with a screaming brat
                on each hip, while you go gallivanting across London!
                You tell me you're away on business, when all the
                while you've been going hog wild in the brothels!

WILL   Never, my love! I am forever faithful!

ANNE   Save it! You have a mistress! Everyone knows about it
                now!

WILL   Scandal!

ANNE   They call her the Dark Lady. Since when did you prefer brunettes?

WILL You are the only one! You are my succulent pomegranate! My shapely gourd!

ANNE Eat worms! I read all about your little hussy in this book of sonnets you wrote!

WILL I wrote no sonnets.

ANNE I suppose you're going to tell me her eyes are like the sun!

WILL Her eyes are nothing like the sun!

ANNE SO I'VE READ!

WILL Let me come home with you to Stratford! I'll prove myself worthy...

ANNE Don't bother ever coming home! You are no longer welcome in my house! *(stops, noticing ROBERT)* Wait a minute. Didn't you die last year?...Never mind.

> *ANNE leaves, slamming the door behind her. WILL begins to whimper, and slam his head repeatedly against the wall.*

KIT Will, I don't know what to say.

WILL *(thrusting himself into KIT's arms)* Hold me.

KIT   Um, well...

ROBERT   Serves you right. Thou parasite. Thou fungus. Thou involuntary spasm.

KIT   Robert, were you behind this?

WILL   I have no mistress. What means this lady?

KIT   *(reading sonnets)* Robert, these sonnets are written in your hand.

ROBERT   I warned him. He brought this on himself! Yes! I wrote the sonnets! And Shakespeare deserved every couplet!

WILL   What did I ever do to you?

ROBERT   You mock me! With your success! With your humility! Everybody loves you and it makes me want to throw up!

WILL   Everybody loves me except the only person who matters.

ROBERT   OH, smeck up!

KIT   Get out of my house.

ROBERT   You don't mean that.

KIT   Out, scab! *(tossing ROBERT out)* And a thousand times, fie!

WILL   Aye me! I am out of her favour!

KIT   Listen, Will. Why don't you go back to your place and try to get your mind off things. You can write about your fairies. That will make you happy.

WILL   Please don't make me leave. I can't be alone right now.

KIT   What will you do, then?

WILL   Let me stay here with you. Oh, Kit, please! I can't be by myself!

KIT   There's not much room. I mean, since the dead rat moved in...

WILL   *(grabbing KIT's leg)* Only for one night!

KIT   Will, nature calls. Can I leave you alone for ten minutes while I go to the privy?

WILL   Don't leave me!

KIT   I can't very well take you along to the privy. Nine minutes then.

WILL   How can you defecate when my heart is breaking!

KIT   Let go of my leg before I mess my pants!

Exit KIT.

Act One, Scene Nine

INGRAM, NICHOLAS and BLOB are in the bushes. KIT walks by.

INGRAM   Where do you think you're going?

KIT   I'm going to the privy.

INGRAM   The privy?

KIT   That's right.

INGRAM   Then by all means, continue.

KIT   Thank you for your blessing...What are you doing in my bushes?

BLOB   Admiring your lovely foliage.

KIT shakes his head and leaves.

INGRAM   Did you hear that? He's going to the privy.

BLOB   The Queen's Privy Council?

INGRAM   What else could he mean?

NICHOLAS   Why would he be going to the Queen's Privy Council?

INGRAM   It must have been that story we made up about Marlowe plotting treason.

NICHOLAS   Cripes! The Queen must be bringing him in for interrogation. We didn't factor this into the equation.

BLOB   You don't suppose he will rat on us, do you?

NICHOLAS   Of course he's going to rat on us! He is about to be interrogated by the Queen's Privy Council! They will torture him until he spills everything he knows!

BLOB   Marlowe knows everything we've done!

INGRAM   My embezzling.

BLOB   And the Babington Plot.

INGRAM   Bugger off, Blob.

NICHOLAS   They'll put Marlowe on the rack! Quarter him! Boil him! Disembowel him! He'll be sure to blurt something out!

INGRAM   Marlowe is a loose cannon. He must be silenced.

WILL   *(entering)* Kit! It's been longer than nine minutes! Where are you! *(notices spies)* Have you gentlemen in the bushes seen Kit? I don't understand what is taking him so long. I'm rather worried.

BLOB   Keep waiting. He won't be back any time soon.

NICHOLAS   He's being interrogated by the Queen's Privy Council.

WILL   No!

INGRAM   He's being charged for treason and will be tortured into confessing.

WILL   *(rushing back inside)* Fire and Brimstone!

NICHOLAS   What do you suppose we should do?

BLOB   Prepare to be hanged.

Act One, Scene 10

WILL is pacing around in KIT's apartment.

Enter KIT.

WILL   Kit! Oh, Kit, thank God you're okay! You survived! Oh praise be to Heaven!

KIT   Will...

WILL   I want you to sit down and tell me all about it.

KIT   Why?

WILL   Come on, Kit. Give me details.

KIT   It's sort of personal.

WILL   Did it hurt?

KIT   What's that to the purpose?

WILL   It must have hurt. You did a dirty deed.

KIT   You're weird.

WILL   How did it feel?

KIT   I don't know...Refreshing.

WILL   Refreshing?

KIT   As a matter of fact, it felt rather good to let it all out.

WILL   You let it ALL out?

KIT   That is the point.

WILL   I can't believe you did that. And with the Queen watching.

KIT   The Queen was watching?

WILL   Of course. She watches everything.

KIT   Even THAT?

WILL   You shouldn't have done it, Kit. You should have held it in. As painful as it might be.

KIT   It's not healthy to hold it in.

WILL   Tell me this...Did you let anything out that might have upset the Queen?

KIT   To be frank, I don't see how any of this is the Queen's business. A man's... *(gesturing towards his bowels)* internal affairs are private.

WILL   That's not what the Queen says.

KIT   I don't give a rat's ass what the Queen says!

WILL   *(shrieks)* I didn't hear you say that.

KIT   The Queen is a demented woman!

WILL   You are full of crap!

KIT   Not anymore, I'm not!

Enter THOMAS.

THOMAS   Kit, you forgot to empty the chamber pot again.

WILL   Chamber pot?

THOMAS   Must you forget to empty the chamber pot every time you go to the privy?

WILL   The priv...*(hides his face as he leaves)* Excuse me.

THOMAS   What's with him?

KIT   I don't know, but I learned a little more about the Queen than I needed to know.

THOMAS   Never mind. Just empty this chamber pot. I'm not doing it.

Exit KIT with chamber pot.

THOMAS   *(to rat)* Can you believe that guy, Stiffy? He never empties the chamber pot. I'll bet he does that on purpose just to irk me. That is so like him.

Knock at the door.

OFFICER 1   Open up in the name of the Queen!

THOMAS opens the door.

THOMAS   What the...

OFFICER 2   Christopher Marlowe?

THOMAS   The name's Thomas Kyd.

OFFICER 2   Is this the residence of Christopher Marlowe?

THOMAS   He's my roommate.

OFFICER 1   Search the premises.

THOMAS   You can't come in here! This is private property!

OFFICER 1   We have a search warrant from the Queen.

OFFICER 2 finds Atheist literature in the closet.

OFFICER 2   I found something!

THOMAS   What?

OFFICER 2   Brochures of an Atheist nature. Along with some heretic accusations signed by one Richard Baines.

OFFICER 1   Do you know anything about this, Thomas Kyd?

THOMAS   I don't know anything!

OFFICER 2   He knows something. Take him away!

>   *OFFICERS grab THOMAS and drag him out. THOMAS begs and screams "It was Kit!" repeatedly on the way out.*

>   *END OF ACT ONE*

Act Two, Scene One

> *KIT enters the apartment. THOMAS is not there. He finds STIFFY lying in the middle of the floor.*

KIT   Stiffy? What are you doing here all alone? Thomas never goes anywhere without you...Something isn't right.

> *Door opens. WILL helps THOMAS walk in. THOMAS is in a full body bandage with only his eyes and mouth exposed. THOMAS walks in stiffly and with great difficulty.*

KIT   Thomas?

THOMAS   Kit, before you do anything to me, let me remind you that I am in a tremendous amount of pain.

KIT   I hate conversations that begin that way.

THOMAS   I would also like to say that I love you...in a purely platonic way.

KIT   What did you do?

THOMAS   Do? I, um...

WILL   He told the Queen you are an Atheist.

KIT   Thomas! Have you taken leave of your senses?

THOMAS   I didn't mean to, Kit! It just sort of slipped out while they were torturing me!

KIT   Do you know what they do to Atheists?

THOMAS   Um...the same thing they just did to me now?

KIT   Thomas!

THOMAS   They tortured me! Nearly to death!

KIT   Perhaps I should send you back so they can finish the job!

THOMAS   It's not as though they tickled it out of me! They put me on the rack! What did you expect me to say?

KIT   I don't know. The truth, maybe?

THOMAS   I tried the truth! I really did! But the truth wasn't interesting enough for them! They wouldn't stop torturing me until I told them what they wanted to hear!

KIT   What they wanted to hear?

THOMAS   They came here looking for you, Kit! For you! They searched the apartment and found those Atheist brochures we tossed in the closet. And some prank heretic notes that Dick wrote. You weren't around so they took me in to be interrogated. They asked me who the heretic literature belonged to, and I blurted out, "Marlowe! They belong to Christopher Marlowe!"

KIT   I know we've had our differences, but this...

THOMAS   They wouldn't stop until I gave them the right answer! They want you to be guilty! The Queen has it in her head that you are an Atheist, and once that woman has her mind set on something...

KIT   God save me!

THOMAS   They're coming to get you, Kit. *(knock at the door)* There they are.

OFFICER 1   *(from outside)* Open up in the name of the Queen!

KIT   Couldn't I open up in the name of someone else?

WILL   Just tell them what they want to hear. It will keep you out of trouble.

KIT   I suppose it has kept YOU out of trouble, hasn't it, Will?

OFFICER 2   Is Christopher Marlowe in there?

KIT opens the door.

KIT   I'm the man you want. How have I offended the Queen this time?

OFFICER 1   Treason.

OFFICER 2   Blasphemy.

KIT   Which one is it?

OFFICER 1   We'll let the Queen decide that.

OFFICER 2   Seize him!

> *The officers each seize KIT by each arm and begin to take him away.*

WILL   Wait! Don't take him away! *(straightens KIT's ruff and fixes his hair)*

KIT   Will, what are you doing?

WILL   You're seeing the Queen. You must look your best.

> *OFFICERS take KIT away.*

THOMAS   There goes a dead man.

WILL   It doesn't make any sense.

THOMAS   We are all players in the Queen's charade. The only thing we can do is recite our lines.

> *Enter CATHERINE and JOHN.*

CATHERINE   Kitty? Are you here?

JOHN   *(noticing THOMAS' bandages)* New outfit?

THOMAS   The rack.

JOHN   Ah.

CATHERINE   I brought Kitty some homemade mustard and cress juice in case he has scurvy.

JOHN   I told her she was being a mutton head.

CATHERINE   They say scurvy can cause irritability and make people loose control of their actions.

JOHN   If that's the case, Kit was born with scurvy.

CATHERINE   Has Kitty mentioned having any pains in his loins?

THOMAS   Um...Ms. Arthur?

CATHERINE   Have his teeth fallen out?

THOMAS   Kit isn't here.

CATHERINE   Where is he?

THOMAS   He's sort of being...tortured.

JOHN   What did he do this time?

THOMAS   He was charged with possession of heretic literature.

CATHERINE   (*throwing herself on the floor*) I've failed! I've failed!
                I've failed!

JOHN   (*shoving a shoe in her mouth*) Stuff it, Catherine.

Act Two, Scene Two

The stage is dark. KIT is spotlit, centre stage, facing the audience. He has an officer on either side of him. He is being questioned by the Queen. QUEEN is not visible. Only her voice is heard.

KIT   So which is it? Treason or blasphemy?

QUEEN   They are the same.

KIT   What say you?

QUEEN   I am your Queen. If you reject God, you reject me.

KIT   I believe in God. But I don't believe in you. If that makes me an Atheist, then go ahead and torture me.

OFFICER 1   Treason!

OFFICER 2   Blasphemy!

QUEEN   I will ask you one more time. Are you an Atheist?

KIT   Not exactly.

QUEEN   Are you a Christian then?

KIT   I'm not sure.

QUEEN   Then what are you?

KIT   Confused!

QUEEN   What confuses you? You are either a Christian or you're not. Judging by your less than model lifestyle, all fingers seem to point at Atheism.

KIT   I know there's a God somewhere. I just don't know where to find him.

QUEEN   And you expect to find him in a tavern?

KIT   Why not? I can't find him anywhere else. Everywhere I turn I see blood and gore. Covert death plots. Loveless marriages. Espionage. For the love of Ud, people watch public hangings for fun!

QUEEN   The content in your plays is no better.

KIT   I'm only commenting on things that need to be changed.

OFFICER 1   Shall we hang him now, your majesty?

QUEEN   Let him finish.

KIT   Religion has nothing to do with God anymore. God has been replaced with a monarch. You have shoved God in a closet somewhere and taught us to forget about him.

QUEEN   I am God.

KIT   If that's the case, then you are the blasphemer. Not me.

QUEEN   You will be silenced. I shall have your ears cut off.

KIT   Why would you cut off my ears to silence me? I don't talk with my ears.

QUEEN   Did I give you permission to say such things?

KIT   You are not my puppet-master. I can say whatever I bloody well please without any prompting from Queen Elizabitch. Did I say that out loud?

QUEEN   Nobody has ever spoken to me in this manner. Unprecedented.

KIT   I don't do anything unless it's unprecedented.

OFFICER 1   Shall I call for the rack-master, your majesty?

KIT   Go ahead. I value the liberty of speech above my very life.

QUEEN   Enough of this privy-nip! You will report to court every day until your next date with the Privy Council. Don't leave town, Marlowe. I'm not done with you yet.

OFFICERS take KIT away.

Act Two, Scene Three

The apartment.

THOMAS I can't believe you called her Queen Elizabitch.

KIT I can't explain it, Thomas. I open my mouth and these things just start flying out. It frightens me sometimes.

THOMAS It might be scurvy.

KIT Wha?

THOMAS Your mother was here.

KIT Oh.

WILL How could you say such things to the Queen? What if it offended her?

KIT That is the point, Will.

THOMAS So that's what this was all about. You put on this big performance for the Queen just so you could get a rise out of her. This is so like you.

KIT Thomas...

THOMAS You wanted to see how mad you could get her before she tortured you. Do I know you or do I know you?

KIT Thomas...

THOMAS You always have to push boundaries, don't you, Kit? Challenge limitations. Well, if you're that dumb, you deserve to be tortured.

WILL That wasn't very nice, Thomas.

KIT I may have a big mouth, but every word that comes out of it is the truth.

> *ANNE is heard screaming outside the door.*

ANNE *(from outside)* Did I say you could touch me?

ROBERT *(from outside)* You love it.

> *Enter ANNE and ROBERT.*

THOMAS Robert Greene? Wait. Didn't he die last year?

ANNE Touch me again and I'll give you a bloody coxcomb!

ROBERT I'm only taking what's mine.

WILL Yours?

ROBERT There's no point in letting a perfectly good set of knockers go to waste. After all, Shakespeare, you're not using them.

ANNE   Will, do something about this thug, will you?

WILL   I don't know if I can.

ANNE   And they said chivalry was dead.

KIT   Will, are you just going to stand there and let...

ROBERT   He won't do anything. He'd rather choke to death on the milk of human kindness than to stand up to me.

WILL   Mr. Greene?

ROBERT   He's afraid he would offend someone.

WILL   Mr. Greene?

ROBERT   And even if he had any testosterone, he's too much of a moron to figure out a good revenge plot.

WILL   Mr. Greene?

ROBERT   Yes. What?

WILL   Have you ever read *Arden of Feversham?*

ROBERT   The play written by the anonymous dramatist? I know it well.

WILL   Remember that really evil character in it named

Greene?

ROBERT   That greedy, selfish jackass who looks out for none but himself? What about him?

WILL   Who do you think wrote *Arden of Feversham?*

ROBERT   I just told you, it was anonym…You didn't.

WILL   Not bad for an illiterate bard.

ROBERT   You wrote a scandalous play and put me in it!

KIT   Way to go, Will!

ROBERT   First you steal my audience, now my reputation!

WILL   And you stole my wench! *(punches ROBERT in the face)*

                                    KIT, THOMAS and ANNE have identical looks of shock on their faces.

ROBERT   You hit me in the nose!

WILL   I would have gone for the balls, but you don't have any.

KIT   I knew you had it in you, Will!

ROBERT   *(noticing ANNE)* Ug! Get away from me, Strumpet!

ANNE   What the…

ROBERT   I will not touch something that William Shakespeare
                has touched! *(leaving)* You will never amount to
                anything, William Shakespeare! Never! *(exit)*

WILL   *(calling out to ROBERT)* I hope you won't take any of
                this personally, Mr. Greene!

ANNE   You rescued me, my adorable, little Willie Woo Woo!

KIT   Willie Woo Woo?

WILL   She calls me that sometimes.

ANNE   Come here, you! *(grabs WILL by the sides of his head
                and kisses him aggressively on the mouth)*

                                    *WILL looks stunned for a moment
                                    and then passes out.*

ANNE   Not this again.

                                    *ANNE flings WILL over her
                                    shoulder and carries him out.*

KIT   Now THAT'S drama.

THOMAS   Kit! You have darker matters to concern yourself with.

KIT   I don't want to think about it. I may only have a couple
                of weeks left and I want to savour them.

THOMAS   Have you thought about skipping town? Assuming a
                new identity?

KIT   I thought about it. But it's a stupid idea. I am a high profile man. Someone would eventually discover me.

THOMAS   So what are you going to do?

KIT   Stop ambushing me, will you? I just want to get my mind off things. In fact, I've made plans to have dinner with some friends in Debtford Friday next.

THOMAS   You have friends?

KIT   Ingram Frizer, Nicholas Skeres and Blob Poley.

THOMAS   You're not supposed to leave town. Furthermore, do you think it's safe to be seen in public?

KIT   I will be safe as long as I'm in the company of friends.

Act Two, Scene Four

The tavern of MADAM ELEANOR BULL. KIT, INGRAM, NICHOLAS and BLOB are seated around a table.

NICHOLAS   Perk up, Kit.

BLOB   Yeah. You look like death.

BLOB gets kicked from under the table.

INGRAM   The whole point of this evening is to help you get your mind off things. How about a game of backgammon?

MADAM BULL   Wine, Gentlemen!

BLOB   Wine? We want ale, Eleanor!

MADAM BULL   Wine is better for toasting. And you may call me Madam Bull.

NICHOLAS & BLOB   Ooooo. Madam.

BLOB   Not just a wench, but a classy wench.

NICHOLAS   She is practically royalty.

MADAM BULL   Not quite royalty. Let's just say I have court connections.

INGRAM   *(pulling MADAM BULL on his lap)* Come here, Madam Bull.

MADAM BULL   A toast! To cousin Blanche. God rest her soul. *(bursts into laughter followed by the others who do the same)*

KIT   Who's cousin Blanche?

MADAM BULL   She was the Queen's chief gentlewoman and confidante. Good old Blanche finally kicked off and left me in her will.

INGRAM   Ching, ching.

MADAM BULL   That's not all she left me. She also left me in the Queen's favour.

NICHOLAS   To the Queen!

                                    They all raise their glasses in a toast, except KIT.

INGRAM   Kit?

KIT   *(no enthusiasm, still not raising his glass)* Klink.

INGRAM   There's just no pleasing you, is there, Kit? Here we invite you to Debtford for a nice evening of gluttony and drunkenness and all you do is mope. And Madam Bull was so kind as to offer us a room for the enire day for a sum of pence.

MADAM BULL   What do you mean kind? I'm the one who gets to be surrounded by four devastatingly handsome men. *(to BLOB)* Except maybe you.

KIT   Are we here to eat or not?

MADAM BULL   Then there's this one. *(drapes her arms around KIT from behind and talks into his ear)*

KIT   Me?

MADAM BULL   You're my favourite.

> *INGRAM, NICHOLAS and BLOB pound on the table and make animal noises.*

KIT   Madam, please.

MADAM BULL   Where did you get such pretty clothes?

KIT   I'm hungry.

MADAM BULL   So am I.

> *INGRAM, NICHOLAS and BLOB howl like dogs. KIT peels MADAM BULL off of himself.*

KIT   Terrific. Starve me to death. I'll be spared of the Privy Council.

INGRAM   He gets irritable when he's deprived of food.

BLOB   Me too. Food, Wench!

NICHOLAS   *(grabbing MADAM BULL's hindquarters)* She's not a wench. She's a madam.

MADAM BULL   Alright already. I'm taking orders.

BLOB   It's Wednesday. Fish night!

INGRAM   I'll have an order of eel.

NICHOLAS   I'll have the cockle and lamprey combo.

MADAM BULL   Do you want filberts or field mushrooms with that?

BLOB   How are your oysters?

MADAM BULL   They smell a bit off tonight.

BLOB   I'll take two dozen.

KIT   Pork please.

                        Everyone stops and gives KIT a look of shock.

BLOB   But, Kit. It's fish night.

KIT   I want pork.

NICHOLAS   But everyone orders fish on Wednesdays.

KIT   Right. And I'm ordering pork.

INGRAM   Always has to be different.

Exit MADAM BULL.

KIT   I have to pee. *(gets up)* Before I go, I just wanted to thank you guys for doing this for me. I've been an ogre all day, taking things out on you. I don't say this often, so savour it. Sometimes I feel like you guys are my only friends. The only constant thing in my twisted life. There aren't many people who I trust but... Hell. I really have to pee. *(leaves)*

NICHOLAS   Anyone feel guilty right about now?

After a brief pause, they all burst into laughter.

INGRAM   Betraying a good friend makes us all the more skilled as spies.

BLOB   Remember the Creed of Spies?

They put their hands on their hearts and recite in unison.

ALL   A spy is dedicated to the eternal promise to protect, uphold and defend the life and dignities of her majesty the Queen, and to take pride in the loyalties thereof. To live for the Queen. To die for the Queen. Until someone else gives us a better offer.

INGRAM We must follow through with our plan. Marlowe must be killed. Otherwise, he'll surely reveal unflattering information about us when he is being tortured.

BLOB Who will do the deed?

NICHOLAS Blob and I are the most experienced in death plots.

INGRAM Fie! What makes you think I can't do it!

NICHOLAS Ingram, we never said...

INGRAM You don't think I have it in me! You don't think I'm a good enough spy to betray my own friend!

NICHOLAS Ingram, haven't I always said that when it comes to money-lending, you are the devil incarnate?

BLOB You don't have to prove anything to us, so get this chip off your shoulder.

INGRAM I'll prove to you how worthy I am to bear the Creed of Spies. I will do the deed!

NICHOLAS Whatever...

INGRAM I have the entire conspiracy worked out in my head. We will distract Marlowe by starting a heated argument.

BLOB   No challenge there. It's easy to get Marlowe angry.

INGRAM   Who here is in charge of the plot, you or m...

                                          *INGRAM   notices MADAM BULL
                                          nervously skulking about. She is
                                          conspicuously carrying a dagger.*

INGRAM   Madam Bull?

MADAM BULL   Dagger? What dagger?

BLOB   What would a madam need with a dagger?

MADAM BULL   Okay, you caught me. I was going to use this dagger to
                   kill Christopher Marlowe.

NICHOLAS   Whatever for?

MADAM BULL   As a favour to the Queen. She wants him dead because
                   he humiliated her when he was being questioned.

NICHOLAS   Why doesn't she wait a few days and have the Privy
                   Council order his murder?

MADAM BULL   It would make her look bad. After all, Marlowe was
                   once in the Queen's secret service. She'd like to have
                   people think that she treats her employees well.
                   Besides, who knows what scandalous things Marlowe
                   would say about the Queen while under torture?
                   Marlowe's mouth has a mind of its own.

INGRAM   That's for sure.

MADAM BULL   Who's to say Marlowe wouldn't curse and defy the Queen right there in front of everyone? Independent thinkers are dangerous. Others might follow Marlowe's lead and before you know it, there could be a series of treasonous plots against Elizabeth's life. Marlowe must be silenced before the trial.

NICHOLAS   This is such a co-incidence. We were just about to murder Marlowe too!

INGRAM   Me. I was the one who was...

BLOB   This saves us a lot of trouble. Madam Bull can do the dirty work and we won't run the risk being hanged.

INGRAM   You all hate me! You think I'm a mockery to spies everywhere! What reason have I to live!

NICHOLAS   On second thought, maybe you should let Ingram do the deed, Madam Bull. He has some self-esteem issues. It might help him in the healing process.

MADAM BULL   By all means. I'm a sucker for vulnerable men. Would you like to use my dagger, Ingram?

INGRAM   I have my own dagger right here in my stocking.

BLOB   Shhh! Kit's coming!

Enter KIT.

INGRAM   Oh! Am I stuffed!

KIT   But our food hasn't arrived yet.

BLOB   You took too long. We ate already. Yours too.

MADAM BULL   *(caressing KIT's face)* You are such a handsome one. Those brown eyes. It's such a waste. *(kisses him)*

KIT   What means this lady?

NICHOLAS   Someone has to take care of this bill.

KIT   This one's on me, gentlemen.

BLOB   What do you mean, on you? We ate your meal.

KIT   It's the least I can do after the way I've snapped at you.

NICHOLAS   But I wanted to pay for dinner tonight!

KIT   Put your purse away, Nicholas.

NICHOLAS   MAKE ME!

                                    INGRAM creeps up behind KIT.

KIT   I'm trying to be nice here!

BLOB   There will be no niceness in this tavern! I am paying the bill!

                                    INGRAM pulls dagger from his stocking.

NICHOLAS   Take one more coin out, and you'll be swallowing it!

KIT   You paid last time, you bastard!

NICHOLAS   Say that to my face!

> *INGRAM assumes the position to plunge the dagger into KIT.*

BLOB   Give me that bill, you ruffian!

KIT   Your money is no good here!

> *Lights go out. Arguing continues.*

BLOB   You want to take this outside!

KIT   Maybe I do!

NICHOLAS   Why I oughta'...

MADAM BULL   Kit! Look out behind you!

> *MADAM BULL lets out a blood curdling scream.*

Act Two, Scene Five

> *The apartment. THOMAS is still in his full body bandage. WILL is pacing.*

WILL   It's been three days since Kit went to Debtford. Where in the world is he?

THOMAS   It was rather rude of you not to see your wife off when she left for Stratford. You may never see her that amorous again.

WILL   I'm worried here. It's been three days.

> *Enter DICK.*

DICK   Have you heard?

THOMAS   We don't have the patience for you right now, Dick.

DICK   If you give me five ducats, I'll tell you what I know.

THOMAS   That'll take all of three seconds.

DICK   Christopher Marlowe is dead.

> *THOMAS and WILL stop and look*

> *shocked. After a short pause,*
> *WILL begins weeping hysterically.*

THOMAS   What happened?

DICK   Five ducats.

THOMAS   I'll give you five kicks in the head if you don't tell me.

DICK   He was stabbed in a tavern brawl. I don't know all the details, but I hear that it was all Kit's fault.

THOMAS   It always is. You know nothing more?

DICK   Only that the murderer claims he did it in self-defense.

Act Two, Scene Six

The stage is black. In the centre of the stage is a spotlight which illuminates DANBY the coroner, OFFICER 1 and the body of KIT on a slab. There is a sheet over the body with a dagger sticking out of the place where the head would be.

DANBY   Self-defense?

OFFICER 1   That's what the Queen says.

DANBY   But I've read the witness' report and...

OFFICER 1   The Queen says it was self-defense. Don't make her a liar.

DANBY   I am a coroner. Not a miracle worker.

OFFICER 1   Danby, you are the Queen's coroner. Do what the Queen says.

DANBY   Why wasn't the local coroner in Debtford notified? The Queen's coroner isn't supposed to be involved unless the murder took place within twelve miles of the

Queen's person. The Queen was at Nonsuch Palace in Surrey the night of the murder.

OFFICER 1 Stop asking questions. Just have something intelligent for the trial. We need a coroner's inquest.

Exit OFFICER 1.

DANBY I am a dead man. This witness' report is full of inconsistencies. There's no way this could have been self-defense. Come on, Danby. Think of something.

Lights change colour and DANBY is at the trial.

DANBY Gentlemen. I have prepared the coroner's report. The murder weapon cost twelve pence.

OFFICER 1 The body, Danby.

DANBY Yes. The body is dead.

OFFICER 1 Danby, your testimony?

DANBY *(deep breath)* The dagger, belonging to one Ingram Frizer, entered the victim's brain through the entry of the right eye. I know what you're thinking. How could this be done in self-defense if the victim was stabbed in the face with the murderer's own weapon, which had been moments earlier, sheathed in Frizer's stocking? There is a logical explanation. I have choreographed the entire episode in my head and have come up with what I call *The Magic Dagger Theory*. Since the deed was done in self-defense, we know that Marlowe drew arms first. After a dispute over the dinner bill, Marlowe and Frizer got into a struggle. The magic dagger unsheathed itself from Frizer's stocking, floated through the air and landed in Marlowe's hand. Marlowe, being the AGGRESSOR with the INTENT to kill, used the BLUNT end of the dagger to thwack Frizer on the back of the head. It was not difficult for Marlowe to reach the back of Frizer's head while being pinned down to a bar table, because Marlowe has abnormally long arms and convenient, rubbery elbows.

OFFICER 1   Danby, your story is entirely speculative...I like it. Next witness. Madam Eleanor Bull.

MADAM BULL   He did it! He's the one! Ingram Frizer murdered Christopher Marlowe in cold blood!

OFFICER 1   We'll pretend we didn't hear that. Next witnesses. Ingram Frizer, Nicholas Skeres and Robert Poley.

MADAM BULL   Wait a minute. Ingram Frizer can't be a defendant AND a witness.

OFFICER 1   What do you mean? Our law has no guidelines for evidence. If we do things right, this murder trial won't take more than ten minutes.

> *MADAM BULL exits indignantly. INGRAM, NICHOLAS and BLOB each sit on a stool, facing the audience.*

OFFICER 1   Where was Christopher Marlowe stabbed?

INGRAM   In the eye.

NICHOLAS   In the brain.

BLOB   In the tavern.

OFFICER 1   *(after giving BLOB an odd look)* Where did the murder take place?

INGRAM   A tavern.

NICHOLAS   A brothel.

BLOB   The home of Eleanor Bull.

OFFICER 1   What was the motive?

INGRAM   The dinner bill.

NICHOLAS   A gambling debt.

BLOB   Suicide.

OFFICER 1   Who's idea was it to kill Marlowe?

INGRAM   The spymaster.

NICHOLAS   A rival in love.

BLOB   Some guy named Frances.

OFFICER 1   Thank you, gentlemen. That clears everything up nicely. The final testimony will be from Christopher Marlowe. *(to corpse)* Mr. Marlowe, do you have anything to say in your defense? *(puts ear to corpse)* He has nothing to say in his defense...Now then, what says her majesty?

QUEEN   I am granting Frances Freezer a pardon on the grounds of self-defense.

OFFICER 1   Who's Frances Freezer?

INGRAM   Yes! I got away with it! I am a very good spy!

> *INGRAM stops to find he is getting odd looks from everyone around him.*

Act Two, Scene Seven

The apartment. WILL is alone.

WILL   Something isn't right...Something...

Enter MADAM BULL.

MADAM BULL   Hello?

WILL   Who are you?

MADAM BULL   Eleanor Bull. Who are you?

WILL   William Shakespeare.

MADAM BULL   William Shakepeare? Kit spoke very highly of you.

WILL   He...he did?

MADAM BULL   I brought Kit's hat. I thought someone might want it. I found it in my rooming house the night he was...

WILL   It was your rooming house? You saw what happened?

MADAM BULL   I have to go now.

WILL You know something, don't you?

MADAM BULL I saw nothing!

WILL He was my friend!

MADAM BULL I'm sorry this happened! I didn't know how fond I'd become of...

WILL Was it self-defense? Did Kit try to...

MADAM BULL It was the blunt end of the dagger!...When Kit hit Ingram on the head. He used the blunt end of the dagger. You figure it out.

Exit MADAM BULL.

WILL The blunt end of the dagger. If Kit wanted to kill Ingram, he would have used the blade. Ingram wasn't trying to defend himself. Kit was.

KIT's ghost appears.

KIT Did I hear my name?

WILL Kit! What are you doing here?

KIT Is that any way to talk to a dead friend?

WILL Don't you know it's a felony to conjure spirits? I could get in deep trouble if someone finds you here!

KIT   You did not conjure me. I came on my own.

WILL   Why?

KIT   Will, you are a nice guy. So nice, in fact, that it is quite irritating. Niceness offends people in this backwards world. But people like to be offended. It gives them something to complain about.

WILL   What are you trying to say?

KIT   I wanted to change the world, Will. You do it for me.

WILL   I have so many things to thank you for.

KIT   Whatever it is, your welcome. I have to go.

WILL   Where are you going?

KIT   *(mischievous grin)* Heaven.

WILL   Heaven? But I thought...

KIT   You know how I love to shock people.

WILL   How wondrous!

KIT   One more thing. Look after my mom. She doesn't take things like this very well.

WILL   Go figure.

> *KIT disappears. THOMAS enters with great difficulty, still in his full body bandage.*

THOMAS   Did I hear voices in here?

WILL   Thomas! You'll never guess what I just saw! I...

THOMAS   What? You saw what?

WILL   A spider. I saw a spider run across the floor.

THOMAS   Try not to get too excited, Will. You wouldn't want to overexert yourself.

> *CATHERINE and JOHN can be heard outside the door. CATHERINE is wailing and weeping.*

JOHN   *(from outside)* For the love of Ud, Catherine! Would you stop being so dramatic? You're creating a spectacle!

> *Enter CATHERINE and JOHN. CATHERINE throws herself on the floor.*

CATHERINE   My baby boy! My baby boy! My baby boy!

JOHN   Smeck up, Catherine! You must have seen this coming!

THOMAS   Marlowe himself couldn't have written a more tragic ending.

CATHERINE   Oh, grief! Oh, misery!

JOHN   *(moaning)* Oh, Catherine. Would you believe she was outside, digging her own grave this morning?

CATHERINE   My adorable baby boy, with his big, brown eyes and squeezable cheeks!

WILL   Ms. Arthur? If I tell you something, do you promise never to tell a soul?

CATHERINE   Starting tomorrow I'm taking an oath of silence.

JOHN   I'll believe that when I see it.

WILL   Kit is not dead.

CATHERINE   What?

WILL   He faked his death and is hiding in a secret place.

CATHERINE   You mean to say...

WILL   He's writing my plays for me now.

CATHERINE   Kitty is not dead?

WILL   You have to be sure never to blow his cover. He's hiding from the Queen.

JOHN   See, Catherine? Didn't I say you were overreacting?

CATHERINE   Oh! Thanks be to Heaven!

WILL   Not so loud! It's a secret!

                                    Exit CATHERINE and JOHN.

THOMAS   Now you've done it.

WILL   Kit wouldn't have wanted his mother to grieve. It was one, little fib for the greater good. Besides, I made Catherine promise not to tell anyone.

THOMAS   Will, if you want news to spread fast, just tell Catherine Arthur.

CATHERINE   *(from outside)* MY BABY BOY IS ALIVE!

                                    A look of terror comes over WILL's face

                                    FINIS

www.ingramcontent.com/pod-product-compliance
Lightning Source LLC
Chambersburg PA
CBHW052013170626
46808CB00007B/2905